4/08

PUT ON A
HAPPY FACE!

By Debbie Wiersma
Illustrated by Samuel J. Butcher

A GOLDEN BOOK • NEW YORK

Western Publishing Company, Inc., Racine, Wisconsin 53404

One summer day Sammy and his dog, Tippy, were walking home from the park. Suddenly Sammy noticed a piece of paper on the ground.

"What's this?" he asked, picking up the paper to read it. "The Precious Moments Circus opens tonight!

"Oh, boy!" said Sammy. "I've always wanted to go to the circus!"

"Woof! Woof!" Tippy barked, wagging his tail.

After they had packed their lunch, Sammy
and Tippy headed for the circus grounds. It had
always been Sammy's dream to be a clown. As
he walked along, he thought about what fun it
would be if he could join the circus.

When Sammy and Tippy got to the circus, the
first person they met was a happy little clown
selling balloons.

"Hello," Sammy said. "That looks like fun.
Do you think Tippy and I could help sell
your balloons?"

"Oh, no," the clown explained. "We only need one clown for this job. I love to watch children smile after they buy my balloons. This is the only job for me!"

Soon Sammy and Tippy met another clown. He was an acrobat. "What are you doing?" Sammy asked him.

"I'm practicing my act," the clown answered.

Sammy smiled. "It looks like fun. Could I try to do that? Maybe I could do your act for you tonight."

"Oh, no," the clown said. "My act has taken years of practice. It's very hard to do. And besides, if I gave my act to you, I wouldn't have a job."

Sammy walked away sadly, but he had to smile when he saw the next group of clowns.

"Hi, there," Sammy called just as a girl clown on roller skates fell on her bottom. "Are you okay?"

"Sure I am," she said, smiling. "When I fall down at the circus, it makes everyone laugh. I practice tripping and falling every day."

"It's our *job* to make people laugh," added one of the boy clowns. "It's the best job anyone could have!"

Sammy waved good-bye, and he and Tippy
went on walking through the circus grounds.
"I wish I could find the best job for *me*,"
Sammy told Tippy. "I want to be a clown, too."

Just then, they heard a *splash*. It came from
behind some bushes.

"Woof! Woof!" barked Tippy as he ran to see
what it was. Sammy quickly followed after him.

Tippy had found a dog who knew how to jump through a hoop—and land in a mud puddle!

"My dog and I could do that trick," Sammy said to the clown holding the hoop. "Do you need any helpers?"

"No, thanks," said the clown, laughing. "All we need is more practice. We're going to do our trick during the show tonight."

"So are we!" called two clowns on a unicycle.

"Oh, I would love to ride with you," said
Sammy. "Do you need another clown?"

The clowns shook their heads. "Thank you,
anyway," one of them said, "but I don't think
another clown would fit!"

"Oh, Tippy," said a very sad Sammy, "the circus opens tonight, and it doesn't look like we're going to be in it."

The sad little boy and his sad little dog sat down and cried.

"All I ever wanted was to be a clown," said Sammy.

"What's this I hear?" asked someone in a big, friendly voice.

Sammy wiped away his tears. A very tall clown was standing right in front of him.

"Did you say you wanted to be a clown?" the man asked as he practiced his juggling act.

"More than anything," Sammy told him.

"Woof! Woof!" Tippy barked in agreement.

The clown laughed. "I think I know the perfect job for you. Just follow this path to the Head Clown. Maybe he can help you."

Sammy jumped up, and he and Tippy ran down the path.

"Hello," Sammy called when he saw the Head Clown.

The man smiled. "Can I help you?" he asked.

"I hope so," said Sammy. "A juggling clown told me that you might have a job for me. I want to be a clown more than anything in the world!"

"Well," the Head Clown said, "there's only one job left, and it's a hard one to fill. How would you like to be the sad clown?"

"Yes! Yes! Yes!" Sammy shouted happily.

That night under the big top, Sammy and his
new clown friends put on a wonderful show.
The jugglers juggled, the acrobats did flips, and
the unicyclists whirled around the ring. Sammy
tried to give some flowers to a little girl clown,
but Babe the elephant suddenly scooped up the
flowers with her trunk and ate them!

Sammy pretended to cry, and the crowd
laughed and clapped harder than ever. The audi-
ence thought Sammy and Tippy's silly, sad show
was the funniest act of the night.

It never bothered Sammy that he was the sad clown on the outside. On the inside, he was the happiest clown in the circus!